The North Wind

The North Wind

For Simon

Because I said so.
Read this and I do
hope you like it.

Love
Kimberly Ann

6, 22, 2010

Written & Illustrated

by

Kimberly Ann

2003-2005

To order additional copies of this book, contact:
Xlibris Corporation
1-888-795-4274
www.Xlibris.com
Orders@Xlibris.com
78410

Facts

Non Truths

&

Day Dreams

INTRODUCTION

The North Wind whistles an ageless message through the tall pines; it carries with it a message of wisdom, solitude, and caution to the bold. Beyond the habitable, attainable places in the mountainous region of McDonough N.Y. are the non-trespass-able places, where even McDonough's lifers would never consider venture.

In the back hills, beyond post-able land, beyond brush, thick with dangerous thorns, it is speculated that there is a point of no return. This point of no return carries on for miles with it's masses of entangled brush. Brush so thick with thorns that presumably one swipe from a springing branch could disable a full grown man.

Stories tell that beyond the point of no return there used to live a group of strange people. Strange people, that listened, lived, and survived by the song and power of the North Wind.

Stories and legends entertain youngsters with tales of wanderers lost beyond the point of no return. Old timers tell tales of the old days, of times, when the whistling wind had then as it still is today; oft times been mistaken for human sorrow. Wild Indians, Trappers, and Mountaineers, had taken the long way around the North Woods for so many years that the trails used by them were firmly tramped into the earth "and are still used". Route 220 goes all the way around, but not through the back hills of McDonough N.Y.

ONE

Not So Long Ago

The North Wind carried its timeless message through the crossroads of McDonough N.Y. The breeze brushed the cheek of a young girl sitting on the stone steps of the McDonough General Store. She was listening quietly to Old Bob. Old Bob wasn't really old, but that's how all the men that gathered on the store porch were called.

On a dozey afternoon in a small town, storytelling on a store front porch was how it was, and is, when everybody shifts into low gear, and sets back to listen.

The young girl sitting on the step hugged her knees. Old Bob the store keep was telling tales of way back. Way back when the McDonough General was owned by Ol Tuck, and was over on the other side of the street. Way back when the town was new.

The young girl listened quietly as Old Bob rambled on about magic people and spooky places. She had seen the tall pines, growing close together, casting shadows of dark green. They overhung the rutted red dirt roads that she and her father traveled on in the old Chevy truck. The stories felt familiar to her. The people and places were like home and The young girl moved her feet in the warm dust pushing an odd shaped stone out of the dirt with her toe.

Old Bob was long of leg and leant his tall frame to his broom in an ancient storekeepers repose. His gaze took in the McDonough four corner. Heat waves shimmered up from hot black tar. Newly painted double yellow lines marked a center line. Double yellow lines of a two lane, now dividing what had once been a one lane road, where green grass had separated rutted dirt wagon wheel tracks so many, many, years before.

In his few minutes of reverie, Old Bob thought about the women of before now, women, of a time when they were prized. Brave, but not brazen, and beautiful, unintentionally beautiful.

Ugh! Old Bob nearly fell over: his broom clattered to the porch floor kicked out from under his elbow by impatient parties not included in his reminiscence. C-mon. Quit day dreamin! The daily porch dwellers, even the ever present shaggy dog put out an impatient whine, wanting Old Bob to get some yarns spinnin.

Oh; I was just remembering how it was. McDonough weren't much in its first days. The whole town was the store, a few farms, fur trappers, traders, and mountaineers. The store was a stop and shop in the middle of no place, the farms, were still being cleared of trees and rocks, with the fur traders, trappers, and mountaineers, stopping for talk, and supplies, for their travels on trails round about of their own design.

Wild and wooly it was. Some things around have changed, but not the rocks. McDonough still has enough rock to build a stairway to the moon. And probably back again. The young girl on the porch steps rolled a dusty stone in her hand and Old Bob continued with the story. About 1920 Or So—Before a town is begun it belongs to itself. Animals wander, plants grow, go to seed, die, or are eaten by animals which follow their own various cycles living and dying. Trappers and mountaineers traversed the trails about the hills of McDonough for many years before a trapper named Tucker sat down in a clearing to rest, stayed, and built him self a store.

When there is one person in a town the town runs itself, but after some time other people got tired sat down to rest and stayed in McDonough. About ten families had settled in the little town. It was the women that caused all the commotion. The men were unaware of what their wives were up to, and having gotten away with spending all afternoon on the store front porch had not gave their wives much thought.

Well! Said Old Bob Way back when: there was some what of a rough spell when our town was new. One summer day a tracker, gone store keep, named Tuck, sat quiet, looking out the big window, one skinny hip perched on the window ledge, polishing an apple on his best washed work apron. About ten families had settled round about the store.

The Hattie's lived closest just across the street. The Hattie's included Old Charlie, Ol Ma, and their sweet little sons Tommy and C.G. Down a lot or so had lived the Peteroskie's. Ma and Pa Pete and their girls. Their two girls Leonesia blond, Rose auburn were an eye full of prettiness and almost of marrying age.

Further out from the store farmers had staked out their acres. Stones pulled from the turned earth and stacked in long rows separated the farms of Coral Phillips@The Old Man, Ol Bene and his wife Mrs. Bene, Old Man Gipson, his bundle of Mormon wives and many children, Shattock newly married and waitin on a first child, the banker without yet a bank Mr. Nightengail, Old Bruer a passel of kids, his ever tolerant wife, and lastly the mail man Old Biros, Old Lady Biros and their large passel of kids.

The women were divided, could not see that each had gifts and that if they worked together life would be smoother for all of them. The quilter's fought the gardener's. the spotless housekeepers shunned the more fanciful women, and faith was the final cut. The women could not accept each others different beliefs.

Nearest the McDonough General Store lived Ol Ma Hattie. She had forever been somewhat disagreeable but since her husband had gone missing she had become more meddling, troublesome, and easy to rile up. Ol Ma was gone beyond beauty, up in her years, long of tooth, and her neighbor down the way was not.

Down the street a ways resided the Peteroskies, a rather casual family. The daughters in this family were two long legged young beauties. The beauties went barefoot, spoke up when something was on their mind, and did not always get in before dark. Ol Ma Hattie took up a hatred way down deep in her soul against what she termed the wayward evils of her street.

Whilst the men folk loitered on the store porch, any women worth looking at was being slowly, systematically driven out of town by Ol Ma Hattie. Sneakily, and ever so sly, Ol Ma blamed all the young and the pretties for her mans bein gone. He had never been the greatest, most attentive, or the gentlest to her but he was hers and she sorely missed him. His habit for seasonal spells, and his past, his disappearances, seemed to have been put back burner in Ol Hattie's memory.

Festering and brewing her hatred grew, and Ol Ma Hattie sicked her dogs, her children, and persistently used any means she could dream up to torment her neighbors. The town split. It was not a fine day. All the free spirited beauties, well at least Leonesia and Rose, packed up and hightailed it to the far reaching safety of the North Woods. Ol Ma Hattie stayed in McDonough mean as mean could be and blaming all her ills on every one else.

Old BoB continued once more with his story. Out on the town square an old dog loped on down the dirt road. Night rover, thought Ol Tuck, to his self. I know the feelin well enough. Sweet apple juice ran down Ol Tuck's chin, after a big crunch, an he wiped at it with the back of his sleeve. Thought I was the only one scoutin out the North Woods, but I aint.

Just the night before, it'ud happened that Ol Tuck had gone out for a night stroll. Ol Tuck had been follerin a good scent trail, was scoutin some clear feminin prints, when a stick snap cracked, an he a squatted down quick, a hidin. Peerin out from back of a scrubby bush he could see a man a little ahead of his self. He looked on in silence, curious to why the man was out here in the dark of night.

The man tripped up, floundered about, and fell flat on his face. Ol Tuck shoved a fist over his mouth, stiflen a fit a histereoic, laughin. The man on the ground rolled over on his side a picken up his head in a listnen pose. By gee: it was The Old Man. What the duce was he a doin?

Ol Tuck hunkered farther down back of the scrubby bush. A woman come out, an not just a plain ole corn fed gal neither. The beauty with graceful stride slipped out from in the trees. She was a beauty. She smiled at The Old Man, a shaft a moonlight showed perfect white teeth. Her auburn hair showed its shine, an the curves of her body were invitin, but mostly her long bare legs made Ol Tuck blink-blink a lot.

The woman helped The Old Man up, he laughed when she playfully brushed at the dirt on him. Ol Tuck bout choked. She knew The Old Man. That old codger been up here before. The Old Man an the beauty was laughin and talkin silly crap. Ol Tuck set right down on the hard ground, he was some stunned. He set there long after they left: an then Ol Tuck just got up, turned about an went on home.

E-HAW and the snap-crack of a whip, brought Ol Tuck back from his dreamin. The mail wagon come a barreling on down the main road. Dust rolled up from in under the wagon wheels leaving a cloud behind as the over loaded wagon sped on out of sight round the corner. Old Biros must be down en out, it bein a day after saterdee night roudies. Old Lady Biros set the middle a the seat. Four axe handles wide she were, there weren't nowhere else for her to set.

Hope they didn't tip over the still this time. Last time the rowdies got crazy, some ov em had a brainstorm to take Bruers hand made corn still home with em. The fools lassoed the damn thing an drug it halfway through the woods bafore the mangled mocheene got caught in some trees and ripped the idiots clean off their horse.

Always somethin, one time Bruer, Shattock an the boys got holt o some explosives an the party felt like swimmin in a bigger pond. So they enlarged Johnny's Hole in the creek makin the swimmin hole a little bit bigger. When the dust cleared an the fools was done playin ducks they staggerd on home. The drunks sobered up to find every southside winda in town blowed out.

Always something: he muttered to his loneself. Ol Tuck slid off from the window ledge, an taking up his broom, went outside to sweep his porch and wait for customers. Customers comin to the store mostly came to spin tales. Livin way out in what felt like the end of the world seein other humans that would listen about yer comins an goins was a look forward to time.

Now comes the courtship. Romancin, Ahhh the love. Oh; don't go anyplace I'll be right back. Customers probly could have waited on themselves, but Old Bob was a wee bit stingy and could slice balony so thin a body could read the news page through it. After carefully counting out his change, and firmly closing the cash drawer, Old Bob handed the customer a paper wrapped parcel tied neatly with white string. He then recommenced telling his tale. Rose sat pondering absentmindedly a the plank board kitchen table. She laid down a heavy sock that she had just finished danderin on the kitchen table. What: she thought, had happened to her life? Here she sat in a dimly lit cabin, a danderin socks for a man she hardly knew. Why just last summer she'd been runnin barefoot in the North Woods. Rose pushed her chair back from the table and went to stoke the fire.

The log just needed turning and she poked it over with a big iron poker. She knelt for a bit in front of the stone fire place watching sparks fly up the chimney. Hot like her courtship the sparks was. She thought about the day that she and Coral had met.

She could still feel warm sun on her hair and feel the soft pine needles under her feet. She had indeed been barefoot, running free enjoying the brush of her best cotton paisley skirt on her bare nekid legs.

Great pleasure lies in the feel of soft pine carpet under bare feet. Pine scent on the gentle breeze of the North Wind, ah there were a perfume and sweet song all a one.

And then of a sudden there was Coral. She saw him first and she stopped to stare at him. He was atop the stone fence balancing on one leg and not doin so swell. He had a basket in one hand and a gun in the other. He'd about got his other foot down an almost had it all together when he'd looked up and come eye to eye with Rose. Coral tipped slowly and swan dived into an evil tangle of blackberry briars.

She'd fished him out of the brambles and took him to the creek to patch him up. They had sat on the damp bank of the Gene close like while she washed him up with soft bits of moss. What a mess he was. She done his arms first and then she had reached for a long nasty scratch on his cheek.

Corals eyes caught Roses eyes an when her fingers touched his cheek, his big hand went back of her slender neck. The first kiss is the dream kiss "Oh So Good". Rose sighed and dumped another log on the fire.

Now in a whirlwind courtship, dazzel eyed at a strikinly handsome, blue eyed man, she'd fallin for the same words men use. "Ill love you forever, an you can have the world. Yor my girl now, Ya listen when I talk,

Yer beautiful cause I love you, and we got all the love in the world". Yah most men do think they are just somethin. Then she had blinked, and when her eyes opened she was Mrs. Coral Phillips.

"Whew" She loved him well enough, but cleanin house, danderin socks, cookin up the food, and well, the waitin was most tryin. Most things went fine that she had to do, but the waitin for him was the worst. What he'd not said when he told her she could have the world, was that he'd be out to the barn while she did stuff in her world. From the break of day to deepest dark she was alone.

When he came in from the barn he was to tired to talk. They did cozy up some at night under the big quilt, he didn't need talk for that, just a kiss back of her ear, now that was real nice. Real nice.

The Old Man in from the barn sat alone at his kitchen table. He turned a letter very slowly in his big hands. His big hands trembled when he read the beautiful handwriting.

My Sweet Coral,

The sun is high, my work is done.
It seems it is time for me to go.
I loved you with a child's love,
A sweet and tender young love,
I loved you then I love you still,
Always have and always will.
Don't forget me. I will miss you.
Love Your Wild Rose

How could such pretty penned curves be so final? Rose had gone. She had stayed lots longer then he expected she would. Seemed like all his life he had been called The Old Man, like he never had a youth. Rose was differnt, she treated him differnt, called him by his name, Coral. Though he was not real young she had sparked him. Now she was gone, and he was once again just The Old Man. His shoulders slumped an he sighed in defeat.

Even brave, self reliant women need more than just a good house and food. Rose had a real tough streak in her, and the Old Man didn't have a clue. Oh maybe he did and loved that resilience right along with all her other womanly features. Any how she had things she had to do and she did them.

Old Bob started looking dreamy again but resumed the tale before he got bumped over or binged in his head with checkers or something.

McDonough is regarded mostly as the rockiest, hilliest place God ever took vengeance on. The path that passed for a road to The Old Mans farm was called Creek Road. The Creek Road was narrow an flat for the most part.

The one hill on the road was very steep and this was the way Rose had to go. Her feet hurt, but she waddled along and kept on walking. She walked slowly, her hands cupping her massive stomach. The strap on her old canvas knapsack cut hurtful into her shoulder, an she shifted it.

The North Woods was only a mile or so away, but for a very tired, very pregnant woman, it was a long, long way to go. The North Wind brushed a cool breeze through Rose's hair, and Rose walked on.

#TOO#

The North Wind whistled shrill notes through tops of the tall pines. The whistling wind seemed to be trying to drown out a regular rift of screams. The horrid screams a cutting the air came from the interior of a very small log cabin. The screams carried away on the wind. Rose was giving birth, it was her first time, and she was alone. Rose needed help badly, but Coral never came.

She had made it to the cabin up in the North Woods, with just enough time to lay down on some dusty old furs, and then her tired, worn out body had seriously begun to labor. When Rose's screaming ended, the new baby's screaming began. Needing sleep Rose put the infant to her breast. And the wind whistled on regardless.

Leaves in the green scrub of the clearing's hedge way hung listlessly in the heat of a noon day sun. Silence pressed making the day seem longer and hotter. Of a sudden there was skittering and movement in the leaf litter beneath the clearings surrounding hedge row. All about the under brush, brown eyes peeked cautiously out.

The baby lay where her mother had placed her before she herself had passed out. The naked baby half as big as she should have grown, lay within arms reach of her mother. Arms reach away was a good thing to be when her mother began to pitch and toss with fever, but safe or not, the baby felt chilled and alone. She kicked her feet and thumped a tiny, tiny heal upon the cabin floor.

Hardly even a noise the little heal thump, but the litter about the hedgerow moved seriously. Dozens of beady eyed squirrels came across the clearing and skittered over the stone step. Ever so carefully the squirrels curled up around the tiny baby covering all but her face with a warm blanket of bushy red tails.

The baby slept safe and warm until afternoon shadows crept about the cabin. She was hungry and whimpered as babies will. From the tops of the trees birds began to sing and shrill. Some of the brilliant colored, fine winged birds swooped about the clearing ducking and diving gracefully. Aroused by the music of birdsong, Rose lifted her baby without qualm from the furry squirrel nest and placed her to the breast.

Birds sang sweetly, and squirrels chattered and scuttled about outside the open door of the small cabin. Pearl latched onto the swollen breast with gusto. Happy Birthday Pearl. Pearl turned her head to listen as the wildlife stirred about and welcomed her into their world.

#THREE#

Instinct not knowledge drove the exhausted woman. Rose tore a piece of cotton cloth from her skirt and wrapped the tiny baby in it, she then crawled clutching her baby close to her breast. Ever so slowly, on her knees she crossed the open place in front of the cabin. Stumbling, falling, and starting, again, and again, Rose crept slowly down the narrow dirt path that led to water.

Rose tore open her dress front, shoved the baby to her breast, and fell to the ground. Water rushed swiftly past the two of them. The baby latched onto the exposed breast and the sick woman turned her face to drink from the streams edge.

The North Wind whistled soulfully through the tall pines. Rose came to her senses. She was lying on the mossy creek bank close to the rushing creek. She turned her head once again to drink from the stream, and then she pushed herself upright. The moss was soft but cool under her hands, and it smelt of green earth, new and yet ancient. The baby was crying, and instinctively Rose scooped her up, and cradled her baby to her breast.

If the woman had had thought at all she would have pushed the infant into the fast running water and been done with it. Ancient bonds bade Rose to protect her offspring. The babies name became Pearl, and she lived due to the fever, delirium, and exhaustion of her mother.

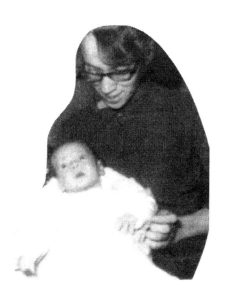

When Rose finally came to her senses she held Pearl close, checked her over from head to toe, and decided to protect this tiny being with her life if it came down to it. Rose and Pearl never had it easy. Staying alive was hard work. Rose took Pearl everywhere with the baby securely strapped to her back in a sling. Gathering food and fire wood is hard work, and twice as hard with a baby tied to you.

Pearl was tiny, about half as big she should have been. Rose doted on Pearl and allowed her to do pretty much what she pleased. Pearl had never grown much, nor had she ever learned to speak. At three years she stood about twenty six inches at full stretch and spoke to her world with wide watchful green eyes. No one in the world knew of her existence other than the birds, the squirrels, and her mother. The North Woods held its various inhabitants scattered about its interior. Busy trying to stay alive the women encased in the realm of the pines rarely crossed the path of another.

Pearl had the good fortune, or super sharp instinct to latch onto a breast, and not let go even in her sleep. For three short years, Pearl's world like herself, was very small. Her whole world was her mother, the cabin, and the creek with its assorted wild life for her playmates.

Brisk was the only thing to call the early morning air inside the cabin. One small grey mouse burrowed down into soft thistle down and slept. The biting air made a body want to snug back into a warm nest of fur. Rose pulled back the covers exposing two faces cheek to cheek. Pearl laughed when she and her mothers warm breath merged making little clouds in the cold air.

Rose sat upon a small stool before the fire place, wrapped in a fur while Pearl perched upon her knee. She dumped some kindling wood on glowing orange coals kept alive beneath a pile of night ash. She and Pearl then watched tiny licks of fire come to life.

Tempting aroma of fried rabbit strips and wild onions filled the cabin. Pearl nursed while Rose waited for her slowly simmering breakfast. Mother and daughter, stomachs full, sat upon the stone step of the small cabin and watched the morning sun rise in a cloudless sky.

Pearl looked up at her mother with big green eyes. She did not have to speak. Pearl's mother having been with her every hour of every day of her life could read her like a book. Yes Pearl we are going to the creek for the day. Stop teasing so!

Time and current steadily take a share of earth, spring season wash is ever swift and strong. Marsh grasses, cattails, and scrubby trees hold the earth firm as best they are able. But down under, where the long roots reach not, hollows form, and thus Rose stepped upon what had just the day before, been firm ground.

The day the ice cold Gene creek took her mother away, Pearl sat on the mossy bank listening to the wind whistle mournfully through the tall pines watching wild birds flit here and there, while her mother floated swiftly down stream.

The North Wind whipped crazily through the tall pines as little Pearl stood alone on the creek bank. Fear, and the fact that she was all alone, scared her, and Pearl cried loud and long. Hours later little Pearl stood alone in the cleared space before the small cabin. The lone babe had cried herself out, and she stood, alone, dry eyed, spent, and silent.

#FORE#

The North Wind tossed and swirled, coming through the town square of McDonough. The wind came straight off the north pines and it carried with it sounds of wailing woman and crying babies. The painted sign on the McDonough General Store swung in the gusty breeze, and turkey feathers adorning a life size carved wooden Indian threatened flight.

Old men lounging in creaky rocking chairs on the stores long porch cussed, as a zealous gust of wind tossed hats from their heads, and checker pieces scattered across the wide plank floor. A small boy in short pants sat upon the porch steps an lifted up his head in wonderment. Thet's a baby a wailin, how's come no one tends it? An old Mormon farmer named Gipson answered the boy in an offhand manner. Aint no baby, boy, it's just the creepin North Wind. Gipson on one knee continued to gather the checker pieces.

Ol Tuck the store keep pushed open the squeaky screen door and came out on the porch. Ol Tuck sat next to the wonder eyed boy an a wipin his big hands on his apron said: Well ya know boy, it's like this!

On a dozey afternoon in a small town, story tellin on a store front porch was how it was, and is, and everybody shifts into low gear, and sets back to listen.

Ol Tuck began with, Well; ya know boy ya got to listen to the North Wind Sometimes it's calm and sometimes whistlin happy, but some days it carries a warnin. Could be of storms or even fore warnins of misery. So ya got to pay attention. Some places hereabouts, ya don't go, and them North Pines is one of em. Peoples been lost up yonder and never come out. Some folk believe they that got lost in there has become spooked. Ya know got spiritual powers and that aint nothin to fool with.

Ya know The Old Man aint been seen in days. Some folk say he went up in them creepy North Woods and fetched him self out a beautiful wife. She weren't right in her head someway an run off ready to birth a babe. The Old Man plumb disappeared last week. Ya know he give her three whole years to come to her senses an come on home. Just the other day he came thunderin into town, rollin up dust on the big brown that he likes so much. Asked me to watch out for his spread for a bit. He looked spooked, like he seen a ghost er somethin. Never even got to answer him back before he tore on out of town back the way he'd come.

Seems to make sense when yer time comes boy find a town girlee an stay outen them woods. Ah Tuck I aint wantin no girlee, gimmee a sodee. The old men on the porch laughed. Ol Bene slapped his skinny thigh and said give the kid a sodee Tuck and bring out some coffee in yer spare time.

#FIVE#

"Night fell the world went black. Today was gone neer to come back.
A star did shine from heaven above. Shining down on the head o my
love. leaves did rustle in gloom tide breeze. Water ran over cold rocks
with ease. Bare feet trod on a well worn path. Brought home my love to
sup and a bath".

Well she weren't trodin no place. She had got washed up the shore
close to home though. That was fact. E Gods the sight to The Old
Man of Rose layin in creek silt and fish muck had took him unsuspecting
for sure. He stood away back from her, mouth agape, the cow switch
trailin the ground, now at its job was done.

Cows are dumb fanciful creatures and get spooky at nitful trifflins.
When his herd had not had a wish o their own to cross the Gene The
Old Man skirted about the long path up in behind the lumberin, bellerin,
beastes, and had spaped a green snap onto their nonwalkin backsides.

He seen her after the fact as the ladies hustled ungracefully up the opposite creek bank. Seen her from where he was still a stompin and bellerin at his unappreciable herd. Even bein whitless the cows had done their best not to trample Rose. Though they did kick more muck onto her with their big clunkin hooves. Rose's baby weren't with her and it'ud have to be looked for. Couldn't leave it to the wiles of nature. The Old Man contemplated the situation, concluded it, and followed after the herd.

#SIX#

She was the tiniest child that her had ever seen. Pearl stood alone before the small pine cabin, cautious, watchful, and wary. In her hand she held a small square of cotton cloth. Much like a wild animal Pearl looked like she were about to bolt away. Her wide eyes showed the confusion and terror that she felt. She stood absolutely still, silent, and watchful. If she had not blinked her eyes he'd have thought her an angel.

The Old Man had known when his Rose had left that she could not have gone far. He had not gone to look for her, as she had left of her own accord. When her body had washed up on the sandy shore near his farm he had felt concern for the child, and had gone to look for it.

He'd had no clue what he would find when he had started upstream. Seeing the tiny child, cold, hungry, and alone next to the small cabin made him wonder how many times his selfishness had hurt his woman, and this child.

Leather creaked as the man swung down from the saddle. He did not tie his horse, and it ambled to the edge of the clearing to crop contentedly on some long grass.

He approached the tiny child with caution speaking softly "I am your father child". Crooning, and speaking softly, he tried to reassure her. He needn't have worried for she never moved. She stood silent, holding her only possession, a faded square of cotton cloth. Only her eyes moved, following him as he came closer to her. The Old Man decided to leave her be, she'd get used to him with time. With time. The single thought passed his conscious into the soft of The Old Mans brain and plans for a new future began.

With that he turned to regard the small cabin. Pearl never moved, only her eyes moved, following him as he stooped to enter the cabin. He didn't expect civilization, or any semblance of order; he really hadn't known what he would find. What he did find set him back a pace or two: as well it should have.

The air in the cabin was already stifling at mere midmorning. The small cabin showed evidence of hard times, and though the cabin was rough with absolutely no frills, it was orderly and clean. He stood stooped, his big frame to large in the limited space. She had worked hard to stay alive. He knew this, by just one look at the dim interior, of the sparsely furnished room.

His first impression was one of a woman's touch. In the corner was a bed, and though it was only a pile of softened animal skins, it had been made up. Dried food hung neatly, tied in leather thongs from the ceiling, and flowers, wilted now, had been tucked into the separations in the weathered logs. Weren't much to look at, but it sure said a lot.

A large wooden pail in its place on a stump, was set in the corner back of the door. The water having set to long was now unfit for drinking.

The Old Man poured out water that he had scooped from the bucket. Tepid water splashed back into the water pail. After he had hung the wooden ladle back on its hook The Old Man sat on the cold stone hearth, head in hands, elbows on knees, having himself a good think.

Now he'd gone and done it, got himself in a real hump. Waving a big hand in the air he spoke conversely while looking upwards. Well Boss seems I might need a lot a help here about now.

Well how do ya do? Perched daintily upon a tattered old book, tucked up onto a bit of ledge, sat an itty bitty grey mouse. The tiny varment stared at The Old Man with its beady brown eyes from the other side of the cabin.

The mouse startled and jumped when addressed by the unfamiliar voice. Skittering off to hide, it knocked the book to the floor. A pencil rolled across the cabin floor having been jarred from its placement as a book marker. The Old Man collected up the pencil and book. He nodded to the little mouse and went outside to sit on the stone step.

Sweet Lilac carried on the North Wind. The soft scent breezed into the clearing and then was gone as quickly as it had come. Small creatures watched with curiosity from the underbrush, the actions in the clearing. His head dropped to his chest and he slept.

The North Wind was still, in the tops of the tall pines. When he awoke the clearing in front of the log cabin was empty. The Old Man stood alone in the silent clearing, with an animal fur in one hand, and a worn diary in the other. He leant his big frame upon the cabin wall with his arms folded across his chest rethinking plans. He suspected that the child was close by, scared, hiding somewhere, probably watching him.

His plans had not been certain from the time he had closed his door this morning. He had not known what would come of this trip upstream.

He still was not sure why he felt it was so important for him to be here. How had the woman and child survived? The diary might hold the answer to some of that. He meant to read it later at the big house. The animal fur had been intended to wrap the child against the elements.

He had no idea where his horse had wandered off to with out him. After a bit, The Old Man looked up jerking his chin from his chest. He felt strange as if he'd lost track of time, and where has his horse? The horse was reliable in the fact that it never strayed. He called for it: Shee ah, and when there was no response, called again, somewhat louder: Shee ah.

Unbeknownst to The Old Man his horse had gone home without him. Pearl had curled her tiny fingers into the long hair of the horse. The horse had lifted her up and they'd gone off alone. The horse walked slowly, carefully, instinctively knowing that the trusting little person on his back needed gentleness. Pearl liked the horse it was big and warm, and when she had crooked her finger at it, the horse had come right to her.

The big horse and little girl watched with curiosity over the top fence rail. The view over the pasture fence was fine and was as close as Shee ah would go. Large piles of brush piled carefully next the farm house for winter kindling began to smoke, flame erupted, and then burst into a hot red and yellow blaze.

Halfway from here to town other eyes saw the blaze reach up skyward and heard the roar of fire consuming dry wood. Pounding with fury little black leather hobnailed boots kicked up dust on the trail back to town.

The North Wind began once again to wend through the tall pines. Sitting upon the door step The Old Man opened the diary and began to read. The first passage he read was a bit personal.

I loved you with a child's love,
a sweet and bumbling young love,
I see you in my memory,
sweet, wise, brave, and off beat.
Summer love, that was you,
my handsome hero, you never knew.
I loved you then,
I love you still.
Always have. Always will.

He wasn't sure that he wanted to read anymore about himself from the woman's point of view. He certainly had been callous and thoughtless.

The scent of sweet Lilac carried away on the North Wind. With a half thought that there are no damn Lilacs up here The Old Man's chin touched his chest again. When he woke up he jerked his head up. Where was his horse? Where was that child? He stood up and walked across the clearing. He stopped walking and looked up at the tree line. High above the tall pines, was smoke "curling black smoke". He stood, mouth agape, mesmerized watching the smoke rise, curl, and waft off into the sky.

#SEVUN#

No breeze stirred the air in town, flies buzzed lazily in the hot sun. Bet it's a hundred ten in the shade. The banker Mr. Nightengail wagered to his card buddies Bene, Gipson, and Bruer. Bet its hotter even said Bruer. I got to get on home. Yer wife on yer tail agin Bruer? Bene joked. Yers is right in back of ya an I aint a kiddin ya Bene.

The half dozen men of the McDonough General Store's Afternoon Porch Committee all looked mighty sorry that they'd not packed it all up ten minutes ago and found higher ground. Experienced hands slid cards from tables into pockets. A pack of angry wives, four of them belonging to Gipson, were marching up the narrow dirt road. The angry wives descended upon their recalcitrant husbands. The guilty parties had lounged on the stores porch for most of the afternoon. More than a few of the men slunk along toward home in front of a poking finger and a sputtering woman.

Ol Tuck puttered around in his store until the commotion moved off. Enough woman in the world he grumbled, put tags on one an they own ya, an ya got to let em in the house even. He came out on the empty porch sat in a rocking chair and was about to prop up his feet when he saw the smoke. The chair slammed down and Ol Tuck ran for the fire bell.

The fire bell cancelled all plans the wives had made. Every hand able, and some not gathered at the McDonough General Store. Ol Tuck pointed toward the Phillips spread at the curling black smoke in the sky. Men lucky enough to have horses got on them and rode off to fight the blaze. Everyone else climbed into a wagon or ran but every man went to help a neighbor in trouble.

That looks bad, Yeah that's real bad aint no savin it. Smoke curled and drifted away. Fore children sat on the porch steps taking advantage of the commotion. Each child had a soda and a fistful of hard candy. Wally and a little red headed girl thanked absent Ol Tuck. The little Hattie boy's in short pants did not. Little C.G. Hattie grabbed up a bagful of tobacco and ducked off around the corner of the store. Little Tommy Hattie shoved his thumb in his mouth and ran for home. Once in his favorite smoke spot, hidin from everyone, but mostly from his mother, C.G. sat back and rolled another perfect cigarette.

#ATE#

The North Wind once more whistled calmly as dusk fell upon the clearing. The horse nickered, and snorted, startling The Old Man causing him to jump and spin around. He shook his head again, and dropped the diary, as if it were hot. He felt dazed as though his head were full of cobwebs, foggy cobwebs like those of a half sleep.

The horse nickered again. Shaking his head, the man watched in amazement, as the horse turned its head around to the tiny child on it's broad back. So tiny she was. The little child wrapped her tiny hands in the horses long silky mane, and the horse swung her around and down to the ground.

Something was missing, but awestruck, The Old Man let the thought pass. The little girl laughed, until her feet hit the dirt, and she let go of the big horse. Pearl's head dropped and she was still.

The horse ambled to the edge of the clearing to crop at the short grass. Pearl stood silent, only her eyes moved. The confusion, and terror, that had been in her eyes earlier were gone now, but she once again, stood absolutely still silent, and watchful.

The Old Man bent and picked up the old diary, and the animal skin, he then turned to look at the tiny child. Yer a nymph Pearly, and a very naughty one at that. He pointed the diary at Pearl with a serious look on his face. Yer mother kept a diary Pearly, "and I know".

The North Wind, became quiet, far above in the tall pines. Pearl stomped her tiny foot on the hard earth. The air in the silent clearing was instantly filled with angry, swooping birds. Pearl whistled and the ground in front of the cabin was filled with darting, chittering, ground squirrels. Pearl raised her tiny arms above her head and spun on her tiptoe's round and round.

Faster ever faster Pearl spun, the birds spun in sync in the air about her head, and the squirrels ran round her feet in perfect sequence. Pearl, the birds, and the squirrels, entranced The Old Man with their strange dance, it was really quite beautiful.

Pearly; The Old Man said sternly, while clapping his big hand loudly on the diary. Pearl stopped instantly, and sat down hard on her bottom in the dirt. Her little chin went to her chest, and tears rolled down her chubby baby face. The birds whirred off into the forest, and the squirrels scuttled away to hidden dens and boroughs. Pearl sat in the dust, and large tears rolled down over her dirty baby face leaving wet muddied streaks.

No one had ever told Pearl what to do before, and Pearl was not happy. Anger was a brand new emotion and it began to rear it's ugly head just beneath Pearl's stomach. Pearl clenched her tiny fists.

The North Wind resumed it's song whistling warning, as the branches in the tall pines began to whip and thrash high over head. The Old Man stood stunned wondering what on earth had just taken place.

Cautiously The Old Man took a small step toward Pearl. Pearl's chin came up. The Old Man took one more cautious step in Pearl's direction. A warning in Pearl's big round green eyes; stopped The Old

Man in his tracks. As the North Wind whipped through the tall pines, Pearl's big green eyes again flashed warning.

The Old Man lifted a foot. Pearl's tiny face tipped up, and an oversized red squirrel let loose a green pine cone. The pine cone struck The Old Man hard; square between the eyes. The big man fell hard: landing flat on his back. The diary flew from his hand and landed about four feet away. Night descended and the world went black.

#NINE#

The wind a comin off the North Pines was fierce, an it was a whipin dirt an old dead leaves at Ol Tuck. The gusts were so strong that when he was a closin the store up, he had to use both hands to pull the dern door shut. He slid the iron bolt home, an then he had to turn an chase his hat, which had blown clean off and was not even travlen in his intended direction. Ol Tuck muttered to his self in some interesten language about long days and ruined plans.

How the blazes was a body supposed to get to where he wanted to get to. Damn North Wind was forever a whippen dirt in his eyes and wreckin his plans. He'd just left the store an already he was bent bout to crawlin.

Ol Tuck left the McDonough General Store an fightin the wind headed up the dirt road for home. Home was not where he wanted to go, and passing Ol Ma Hattie as he went there did not improve his mood.

Mutterin, cussin, and swearin that she kicked extra dirt in his direction, Ol Tuck stumbled up the short path to his home.

The North Wind whipped the house door from his hand: Robbing the misereefied man from even slamming his own door in finality. Old Tuck slipped his apron off over his head. The apron and his hat sailed with a vehemence into the other room. "Blast You North Wind I had stuff to do". Not done bein mad at the storm Old Tuck stomped from his sitting room to his kitchen. The stomps were less than twenty so's they did not count for much. The North Wind payed him no mind what so ever, just rattled the window glass and ripped some shingles from the roof.

Used to be he would track out a woman just whenever he felt like it, but as of late he had 'unawares' got an eye for one beauty. In his mind she was even his girl. Not out loud yet though to no one. Old Tuck was still the tracker—not the trackee. He'd been looking to see her at The Old Man's farm today. Had to look in on all them dumb animals anyhow. All day she had been a buggin in his thoughts. Mebbe she might show up on the morrow.

He sure did like her helping him on the farm. Whatever The Old Man was up to he surely didn't have to hurry back. Branches snapped a regular beat on Ol Tucks bedroom roof. Music of the North Wind drew him off to dream land where all women had long shining blond hair.

#TEN#

The North Wind whistled it's ageless message through the tall pines as first morning sun crept across the clearing. The suns rays illuminated the clearing before the small cabin.

The morning rays fell upon a strange scene. The Old Man lay in the center of the clearing flat on his back. One of his eyes was swollen shut and was very blue black. His one good eye was firmly fixed upon an extremely large squirrel. The squirrel squarely perched upon The Old Man's chest, calmly twirled an oversize green pine cone in it's paws, while it watched him wake up.

Pearly: call yer damn squirrel off before it becomes lunch. A shrill whistle cut the air about four feet from The Old Man's head. The squirrel leapt from The Old Man's chest digging in with sharp hind claws. Gees: his whole body ached, he rolled over slowly. He guessed that he'd only laid on the ground for one night, but it felt more like ten.

From his one good eye he could see Pearl. She was standing on the diary. He needed that book and it occurred to him that if he did not get it he might never leave this place

Pearl stood on the diary. She was so tiny that both feet fit upon the worn leather cover of the book. Pearl's chubby little face was turned up. Her eyes were closed, and she was grinning. Pearl slowly raised her tiny arms hands palms upward to shoulder level. The suns ray's, glinting from Pearls golden curls did make her look like an angel.

The Old Man starred at Pearl perched on his only map out of here. He must have blinked for in an instant, a ball of fire came straight for his face. The ball of fire shot over his head singeing his hair. He rolled for safety as another ball of fire came straight for his face.

Pearly: You are a very naughty little girl, and The Old Man dove for the diary. With one large hand he scooped Pearl to his chest. He had no idea how many powers she possessed, how powerful they might be, or if she even knew what she was doing? He did know the diary was vital. He grabbed it and held it out at arms length. Pearl began to squirm and she whistled loudly. Her whistles pierced the air.

The Old Man ran blindly for the cabin. He couldn't see anything with the sudden mass of birds flying and diving at his head. He didn't feel bad at this point about stomping on a few squirrels in his rush for the door. He hit his head on the top plate of the door and swore loudly as he fell into the small space. He sat in the center of the small cabin, with blood streaming down his forehead. He kept a firm grip on the strange child, and the diary while he kicked the door shut with his heavy booted foot.

Pearly it is sure to me that ya aint going to be a help. The Old Man put the diary up on a ledge near the door. He held Pearl with his big hands pinning her little arms to her sides. He held Pearl out in front of him. She stared back at him from arms reach away. He spoke directly to her scowling little face, Ya aint a goin to like this Pearly.

He spoke to her firmly as he rolled her tightly into a very large fur. Only her little blond head stuck out of the roll and the old man wondered if even that much of her should be free.

Whatever happened with her head out he'd have to take a chance. He sat upon the free end of the roll to be sure that her head remained the only menace to him for the present.

Pearl was stuck for now and could only glare at the old man with her large round green eyes. He took the diary down from the ledge, stretched his long legs out, opened the book, and began to read.

Rose's private thought written in long hand on old tattered pages did give him some insight. Rose had written in the diary of her fears about being alone and giving birth. She had been alone long before she had come way up here.

He had not paid her enough mind and now he couldn't fix that. Well she never said nothing, and he sure as hell weren't no mind reader. He placated him self. Rose had written of her plans to leave the farm. He had thought that it was her wish to go away and stay gone. Pearl was some kind of magical baby, a special kinship child, that was only safe up here in the back woods.

Rose had written of Coral's attitude. What attitude! I aint got no attitude. The Old Man read on. Coral can not understand the seriousness of this birth. He is not listening and being a man what could he know of special kinship any how?

The Old Man fidgeted, and he muttered to himself as the truth sunk in about his deficient listening skills. He recrossed his long legs and read on. Coral has gone off to finish his morning chores. I have cleaned this house from back to front for the last time. His lunch is laid out on the kitchen table and I am on my way out. I hope the cabin in the North woods is still livable. I was born there, and if I can get back to it, this baby will be born there as well.

The Old Man patted Pearl on the head as his thoughts drifted back to the day when he had come home to an empty house. The day that his Wild Rose had left, he had begun to work twice as hard. He was always looking over his shoulder expecting to see her there with him. She was right he had ignored her, but what did she expect; courtin time was for fun, and silly stuff, not after they was married. He was thinking everything was swell; Rose had oddviously not thought the same as him. He had been busy running his farm and now it wasn't worth a bean.

Pearl had fallen asleep tucked up securely in the roll. The Old Man closed the diary and buttoned it up inside of his shirt for safe keeping. He was ravenous so he quietly left the cabin to find food, wood to cook it with, and to fetch water. A water bucket hung on a wooden peg driven into the side chinking of the cabin. He lifted the heavy wooden bucket down.

The unfortunate squirrels that he had stomped in his rush for safety lay on the path where they had perished. The Old Man filled the bucket with squirrels and walked down the narrow path to the creek.

To bad the big squirrel was not among the dead The Old Man pondered to himself as he skinned and washed the meat. That one damn squirrel would be a meal by it's self. And maybe the claw marks on his battered chest might feel better. He sure was beat up in the couple of days since he had got here. No wonder Rose was dead; how had she managed for three years alone?

He wanted to be nice to the child, but the only safe place for her seemed to be wrapped in the big fur. She had to be let out sometime. In the course of two days this tiny little girl had stolen his horse, hypnotized him, and knocked him out cold which left him with only one good eye. She had thrown fire balls at him and singed off some of his hair.

The revelation hit him so fast that he almost fell into the creek himself. The smoke in the sky! If he went home would he find only the missing square of cotton cloth? He put the meat into the bucket filled it half full of water and hurried back up the path to the cabin.

The North Wind whistled through the tall pines, birds sang sweetly, and squirrels chattered as they scuttled about in the clearing in front of the small cabin. The Old Man stood on the stoop in front of the closed cabin door. He had a wooden bucket in one hand, an arm load of wood stacked on his opposite arm, and he wondered if it was safe to open the cabin door or if he even wanted to?

The Old Man cautiously pushed open the door, bent his big frame to save banging his head, and entered the cabin. Pearl was awake, but she was still wrapped up in the big fur where he had left her. He dumped the wood on the hearth stone to one side of the fire place. He started to build a base for a fire and was about to light the kindling when Pearl began to whimper.

Pearls little tear streaked baby face peering out from the roll of fur coaxed The Old Man to set her free. He did unroll the large fur, but not before he propped a heavy chunk of wood firmly against the door. He stoked up the fire and then made up a soup of the squirrel meat. He threw some herbs and vegetables into the pot. He used some of the food stocks that Rose had gathered, dried and preserved. He thought about the food as he stirred it. His stuff, Rose's stuff, finally mixin together, to feed a kid, "their kid", a mix a him an her, that they coulda been raisin together.

While the soup simmered in the iron pot over the fire he sat back once more with his back to the wall and read the diary. His Wild Roses words surely weren't written to make him feel like any hero. I miss Coral. He was steadfast, though not striking, or a converser. The baby was born here in this cabin in the middle of God's land. Blessed nowhere I call it. Sweet Morning Dew is her given name, I call her Pearl.

She is of special kinship as my senses forewarned me. I cant go back down to Corals farm now. The trip to this cabin nearly got the best of me. All that climbing and crawling around took the starch clean out of my bones.

The last mile or so Pearl was determined to be born. She was born in the cabin and that is a relief. Special kinship babies need to be born someplace where it is easy to get to and get there quick. The birth place will be the only powerless place. The Old Man looked over at Pearl playing quietly on the pile of furs. Pearl had found a small lidded box and was happily dumping out it's contents.

The Old Man stirred the soup and went back to reading.

The babies name is Sweet Morning Dew as was prophesized, but I am calling her Pearl because I am her mother and I want to. The trip and the birth without a rest in between nearly killed me. For about two weeks I don't remember to much. I remember mostly the pine song calling me along to do what I had to do to live. Pearl showed her first gifts on her first day when she made friends with the small animals in the clearing. Those little birds and squirrels came right to her from the start.

Pearl screamed and The Old Man jumped up. She had pinched her tiny fingers in the lidded box. The Old Man scooped her up and squashed her to his chest while he examined her tiny fingers. Pearl was alright but in the future he bridled himself he had to pay closer attention. Pearl took The Old Man's heart and wrapped it tight about her little finger.

He reached over and picked up the box. The box was empty its contents strewn about the bed. He turned the box in his hand, it was an interesting weave of inner tree bark The narrow lengths of bark were braided and twisted to form a square box. The cover was a dark knotty piece of bark. The top was fitted with tiny wooden pegs driven through leather pieces this held the lid to the base.

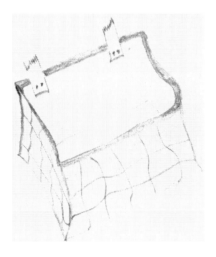

Pearl sat on The Old Mans knee listening and watching all he did in rapt attention. He spoke to her gently as he took out his pocket knife and cut the hinges at the back of the lidded box. Is this yer toy box Pearly? It is now but cha can hev yer lid back when yer bigger. He placed the cover on a high ledge for safe keeping. Put yer treasures in the box Pearly we need to eat.

The Old Man placed a bowl of soup on the floor in front of Pearl and rapidly began to make progress on his first meal in two days. Pearly what er ya doin? Two tiny feet were ankle deep in the soup and ten little toes wiggled on the bowls rim. He laughed as he gently picked Pearl up and set her on his knee. Pearl ya just got to be bout starved. Rose had been dead for at least three or four days.

Pearl looked up at The Old Mans face with a puzzled look. He waved a spoonful of soup close to her face and opened his mouth really wide. His dramatics worked, Pearl copied him opening her tiny mouth wide and he put in a spoonful of soup. He spoke softly to Pearl coaxing her to eat. He had no way of knowing that she was a breast fed baby and had never eaten solid food. Once she got a start on it Pearl was a bit like a baby robin, a very hungry little robin. Slow down Pearl ya act like ya never et before.

Pearly ya know that ya gotta be washed. Yer a dirty little gal with soupy feet. Are ya gonna be a good girl when we go down to the water? Pearl gave him no answer. The Old Man stacked the soup bowls and his own spoon in the bucket. Pearls spoon was nowhere to be found. With the tired baby wrapped in a fur and a bucket full of dirty dishes he left the cabin crossed the clearing and went down the path to the creek.

The North Wind whistled through the tall pines ushering in the night. Stars shown like radiant diamonds in the black night sky. The Old Man and Pearl sat on the mossy creek bank in the moonlight dangling their feet in the cool water. The Old man washed the dishes while Pearl played happily in a shallow pool.

There was no hurry. When Pearl began to look a bit blue The Old Man wrapped her in the fur and the two of them sat on the mossy bank of the Gene. Just remember the Red River Valley, and the one who has loved you so true, played on an old tin harmonica, in harmony with the music of water over stone while he rocked the tired baby to sleep. Pearly he crooned you really do look like an angel, when you are asleep.

#ELEVUN#

The North Wind whistled gently through the tall pines. Birds and squirrels came awake with the sun as morning light swept the night from the clearing. Pearl sat upon the cabin step dappled in sunlight. She whistled a nonsensical tune to herself while she piled small stones on the edge of the step.

The Old Man stirred the fire back to life, adding small sticks to hot coals that had been kept alive through the night under a blanket of ashes. While he worked he pondered aloud his plans for the day. I got to get down to the farm. I have been gone way to long. But what the duce am I gonna do with Pearl. Her ma said she aint safe no where but here.

While the leftover soup heated up he read more of the diary. Pearl played quietly on the door step. So sweet she was just a playin there with the sun on her hair. Her tiny little fingers placing small stones in neat piles all around the steps edge.

Roses entrees in the diary were short but clear. Only girl babies have gifts. No two babies are ever alike. Same as anything. Their gifts are different and so is the degree of power. Pearl's powers are quite strong an new gifts come along real often. Pearl's powers probably wouldn't be so strong if she didn't inherit Corals fierce temper, and then she got his quick wit to go with it all. Pearl communicates with birds and squirrels.

I got that one figered out real fast Rose, ya shoulda writ that one out in big print page one, outside cover even. And she does this strange thing with stones. She makes these little piles of them in a circle around animals an such, an they're trapped inside of there. And whatever is trapped inside isn't a going anywhere till Pearl says it is.

The Old Mans head popped up. Pearl was not on the door step! With panic in his voice he called out. Pearly: Where ya at? Pearls little blond head peeked at him around the door frame. Move yer stones Pearly its time to eat.

Pearl smiled and shook her little head. He put the diary under the far end of the bed and pushed himself up from the floor. He had a real strong feelin that he wasn't goin noplace none to soon.

The Old Man ladled soup talking to himself as he did so. Pearly may have some off the wall powers but I got one of my own. I am the cook an unless she can live without eatin I have a power a my own. He sat back against the wall, calmly ate his soup, leaned back, and went to sleep.

Screaming woke The Old Man. AAAHH AA . . . . Pearly . . . . Pearl was sitting in front of the fire holding her hands out and screaming. The Old Man wrenched from a deep sleep, grabbed Pearl and raced for the creek. Pearl had tried to feed herself and had burnt her tiny hand.

Without thought The Old Man dove off the creek bank. He and Pearl went down under the ice cold water. He sat on the Gene creek bank, holding Pearl on his lap, he rocked her gently, as his tears dripped on her baby fine hair. The Old Man became Daddy.

#TWULVE#

The North Wind whistled an ancient song whispering notes of wisdom through the tall pines. The Old Man stood before the cabin nursing a sore backside. The spell Pearl had cast with her little stones had knocked him on his "well". He didn't know how he'd gotten out of the cabin, but when he'd tried to get back in "damn" the force had knocked him down hard. Pearl was asleep, and he had other things to think of for now. Pearl's little magic stones would have to wait.

Small insects chipped and buzzed, hidden down under sun warmed leaves. The long winding flower scented path seeming endless to the common human eye. Pearl slept on her fathers arm rocking gently with the motion of the big brown horse. Guiding the horse with a caution The Old Man carefully wend his way out through the twisting tangles guarding the treasures of the North Wood.

Shee-ah sensing home was near stepped it carefully down the Creek Road. The gentle brown horse lifted and placed her delicate feet with a caution in the narrow grass lined rut that was the creek road.

Golden tassels bobbed in the gentle wind. The tassels, seed pods of six foot long wild grasses, danced in the breeze. Prickly brushes of lavender bull thistles flowed in unison, along with the not so pretty pesty burrs of McDonough burdock.

Expecting to see all as he left it The Old Man went a bit shocky when he got home. Home was not where he had left it. A zealous gust of wind puffed up a twirl of ash where home used to be.

The Old Man sat astride his horse, his mouth hung open, and he just stared. His house had not been a fashion statement, but it had kept the heat in and the cold out. He looked down at Pearl and tightened his grip. With Pearl tucked safely under his arm he swung down form his horse. He headed for his barn.

Pulling open the red barn doors he entered the cool quiet world of his farm. The inviting smell of clean new hay did greet his nose. His animals were alright, surprisingly not very hungry. He could do nothing with Pearl under his arm. So he rolled her up in a horse blanket and propped her up in a large milk pail. Pearls little blond head turned as she watched him do chores that it seemed were not so long overdue.

Horses, cows, pigs, chikins, a goat, and a pair of sheep were mighty glad to see their keeper. They called out to him in their various voices. He answered them as he worked, mumbling his plans about how to move them all to the cabin. Wagon wont work in the trees, or up the creek. I'm gonna try the winter sled on the creek bank.

With that; he lifted a heavy horse harness from its peg on the wall. Bells jangled as he hoisted the leather harness to his shoulder and left the barn. The jangling bells sounded foolish on the summer air, where on a crisp winter day they had been cheerful.

Pearls head turned and she smiled as The Old Man went out the barn door. When he was out of her sight Pearl giggled. A little face peeked around a bale of hay and giggled back at her.

A mothers gentle hand quieted the giggles coming from behind some musty bales of hay. The mother shushed at her child reminding her that she had to be quiet or stay home next time and not see wonderful funny Ol Tuck. The child quieted and reaching up lifted a straw of hay from her mothers long blond hair.

The riding horse rolled its big brown eyes and stamped its feet not caring for the bells or the heavy harness. The Old Man stroked the horses neck and speaking gently made illusive promises to the horse about a quick easy trip upstream. The horse calmed down and was led around the barn. It followed the man around the barn until it bumped into him and almost knocked him over. The Old Man had stopped abruptly, and stood stock still watching Pearl.

Pearl danced and twirled about leading a strange entourage. She was playing a follow the leader parade with the with his prize white nanny goat in the lead. With the rest of the stock a following along behind her. Was she imparted with circus trainer blood to go with everything else.

That group is a following her like they'd done it their whole lifetime. Cows, pigs, sheep, ducks, an squawkin chikins a taken up the end. The Old Man stood and stared a long time with his mouth agape.

The horse nudged him and nickered in his ear. Yer right he said to the horse. Aint no cause to be surprised, she aint a burnin, bombin, or cagein anything. Lets get the sled loaded bafor she thinks a somethin else.

The Old Man loaded as many bags of feed into the sleigh as would fit. As he worked he tried to estimate how many trips this project would take and if the sleigh did not work: well then what? He muttered and pondered to himself as Pearl played with the animals in the barnyard. When the sleigh was full he tied some rakes and shovels on the top of the load and called out to Pearl. Put the animals in the barn Pearly; come along now; its time to go home. Pearl smiled and shook her curly little head.

The Old Man pressed his forehead to the warmth of the horses neck. He closed his eyes. He needed Rose and what was left of her "the diary" was arms reach into a cabin that he could not get into. Pearl was not safe outside the realm of the tall pines.

The Old Man muttered to himself they might have to stay here if Pearl kept goofing around. The Old Man sorely regretted not having read further into the diary about what and why Pearl might not be safe down here.

Pearl whistled softly. The Old Man turned his head slowly, resting his ear, rather than forehead, to the softness of the horses neck. Pinched between Pearl's tiny thumb and forefinger, Pearl held a small square of faded cotton cloth. The cloth held between her fingers, and at arms length fluttered as Pearl whistled through the cloth. The cloth fluttered gently.

The Old Mans eyes became heavy, so tired, he just needed a little rest. The faded cotton cloth ceased to flutter. Pearl crooked her tiny finger at the big horse. The smell of sweet Lilac wafted away on the North Wind.

#THERTEEN#

The Old Man stumbled tripping over a large root sticking up out of the narrow path. Seeing the world through sleep glazed eyes he regained his balance closed his eyes and went back to dreaming.

Dreamland has its own rules, and oddities are the norm, so when in his dream Pearl was older, and had brown hair, it did not cause him alarm. The fact that he was meandering up the narrow path next the Gene creek, nor the prickling knowledge that he was stumbling along in his sleep following a child bothered him not one iotee.

Soft long blond hair brushed across The Old Mans cheek. A sweet voice crooned to him, gently lulling him, comforting him into a deep sleep. Peaceful sleep engulfed him and he dreamt of soft caring hands. Hands like those of his long lost Rose. Soft hands pushed the hair from his forehead. Soft hands tucked soft covers round tight. Sinking, sinking, so softly into the depths of the other land. Pure unruffled sleep enveloped the man.

#FORTEEN#

Pearl and her first best friend stood quietly in the clearing. Pearls new friend was older but not wiser than Pearl, and Pearl easily outranked her friend in wit and use of power. Like children anywhere status and hierarchy are important. Always, there have been leaders and followers.

Pearl and her new acquaintance stood in the clearing. Pearl tiny, blond hair, light skin, and Aurianna a bit taller than Pearl, dark hair, and skin tanned to a deep brown, stood staring each other down, green eye to brown. Pearls new friend bowed her head in unspoken defeat, and Pearl taking her first action as leader, grabbed her little friends hand, and they skipped away down the path to the creek.

#FIFTEEN#

The Old Man rolled over in his cozy sleepy dream world and came awake instantly as Pearls lost spoon jammed him in the ribs. He sat up bleary eyed not knowing where he was and feeling panicked about being stabbed in his sleep. His vision cleared and he realized that he was in the small cabin. He rubbed his sore ribs and tossed Pearls spoon from the bed.

The metal spoon clattered on the stone hearth. Someone had lit a fire and had started food cooking. The Old Man hoped that he'd not done this in his sleep but then he hoped to hell Pearl hadn't! She was worrisome enough without that.

It was broad daylight and something was scratching up a storm on the cabin roof. The Old Man got up and went out into the clearing to investigate. The cabin door slammed shut startling a dozen chikins on the cabins roof. The chikins flew straight up and straight back down as if dancing upon puppet strings. The Old Man laughed, Pearly could not be far away.

#SIXTEEN#

Two little girls sat side by side on the mossy creek bank. Pearl whistled a whimsical tune and a large rainbow trout swam up to the shallow waters edge. Pearls little friend then clapped her tiny hands, the big fish jumped up out of the creek, flipped in the air and splashed back into the water. The little girls laughed, and rolled around on the cool green moss. Speech was unnecessary, they were having great fun.

The Old Man seemed to stand about gaping in amazement a lot as of late. This time he had heard Pearl laughing and he'd gone down the path to the creek to see what she was doing. Two little girls sat side by side under a shade tree on the creek bank. Hand in hand the two little girls looked shyly up at him. He stood staring, mouth agape, stupidly, looking lost, and then he started to look as if he might bolt and run. Pearl was enough! And now there were two: maybe more? He had not considered any other children than Pearl, but Rose had mentioned other babies in the diary.

The Old Man sat down beside the path on a stump to think. Neither of them should be down alone by the water, and where did Pearl find her friend? He muttered and pondered aloud to himself for a bit. Then something weird crossed his mind: What if? Pearl weren't Pearl? How could he know what child he had stumbled on first? If that little child weren't Pearl it'd sure explain why she looked blank at him, and why she never talked?

He smelled her before he saw her. The woman scent of his beloved Rose. Her sweet scent carried on the gentle breeze. Then he saw her step out onto the dirt path. So beautiful she was, long of leg, bare foot, and graceful. No need for haughtiness in my gal she's a good woman.

He didn't jump or speak. He couldn't have spoken anyhow for the surprise of it all. It was just as well, he did nothing for he wanted the apparition to stay. She was so beautiful, such a wonderful surprise, that he stared unabashedly with his mouth hung wide open. Corals apparition spoke. Close your mouth Coral, are you catching flies or something?

Pearl and her friend were skipping up the path quite innocently until Pearl saw her mother. Pearl was so happy that she spun about on tiptoe round and round. She whistled and the birds and squirrels joined her in a cheerful but wild frenzy. Pearl spun, whistled, and then in pure happiness clapped her tiny hands. Fire flew from her fingertips flying wildly in all directions. The Old Man and Aurianna hit the dirt. Rose merely held her arms high, and humming an odd tune, created a strange funnel, which sent the fire up into the afternoon sky.

#SEVUNTEEN#

Heat lightenin. Damn what a show. The patrons of the McDonough General Store's Porch Committee gazed in awe as high in the sky yellow-orange fire balls exploded sending out cascades of bright orange sparks.

Heat lightning aint no good Old Bene said to his farmer friend Franky. E yep: Franky agreed pointing his hooked cane at the spectacle in the air. Franky never said much and when he did he was usually correct. Be grass fires tonight. E yep; Old Bene nodded his head in agreement.

Ol Tuck the store keep came out o the porch to see what all the fuss was about. What'ed I miss he said; wiping his big hands on his work apron? The kid in short pants on the porch steps said; Ah Tuck yer to slow the heat lightnin fire show is all gone now.

Aint no lightnin kid its them spookful North woods people. Ya can believe what ya will, but when them ones get wild they can throw fire off their palms. Fire hotter then pure pitch straight from Hell.

Ol Tuck jumped a foot or more when a woman shrieked at him from behind the porch rail. The heads of all the lounging men on the porch ducked down, hat brims lowered in hopes that Ol Tuck would get his dues and Old Ma Hattie would go home. It was not to be.

The angry mother shrieked at Ol Tuck in her loudest most piercing voice. I told you morons on this porch bafore and I'm not gonna tell ya agin (she would) to watch yer language in front of poor little C.G. He's just a innocent kid. He aint no Bastard brat like yer used to and his ears is tender.

She then turned her attention to the party gathered on the stores porch. Smokin, drinkin, and cards out in broad day light. Well I never: (she had). While her attention was bent on attacking the morals of the Afternoon Porch Committee, poor, sweet little C.G. had run off. He had run off to hide behind the store and light himself a stump of a smoke that he'd found. Sweet little Hattie whispered to himself whilst puffin out smoke; stupid ol battle axe.

#ATETEEN#

Pearl had calmed down and was cuddled close to her mother. Rose was trying to explain to Coral what had happened. Coral swung the axe with force and cracked a block of fire wood apart. Rose talked, Coral split wood. The clearing had been quiet with a gentle breeze blowing over, when all of a sudden The North Wind carried on it sounds of shrieking. Coral had a startled look on his face and for a moment Rose's face held concern. Maybe someone was injured, dieing, or even killing someone else?

Rose relaxed and she smiled no one was being killed by wild animals. It was only Ol Ma Hattie on a rampage. Her high, shrieking, foul mouth, carried for many miles rather often. Wonder which boy of hers it was this time, C.G. or Tommy? The torrent was a shrill reminder of why life had to be the way it was. The wind changed direction and peace returned to the clearing in front of the cabin.

Rose went back to trying to explain to Coral her death and resurrection. You need to look at things a little closer Coral. I was not dead on that creek bank. I was knocked out, and mighty water logged. I just spent three days dragging myself back up here. But ya looked so bad layin there. There was sand washin over ya. I nudged yer shoulder with my boot an I got no response.

Her hand went straight to a fading bruise on her arm, as his guilty eyes registered on the spot. Why? He muttered to himself. Why was he so careless? He could have rolled her over, he didn't even dig a hole to bury her. Good thing he hadn't buried her. He felt like a bruit. Damn it; why didn't he ever finish anything or take charge.

Pearly was his first mission. He had fed her, washed her, and now that he liked her he would have to go away. Her mother would take over and he'd have to put Pearly on his list of unfinished business. He didn't want to go anywhere.

Coral stood up and stomped off. He turned back before he stepped from the clearing to enter the North Woods. The chikins were still flying straight up and back down. Rose sat on the chopping block with Pearly curled in her arms. Them with the cabin behind sure was something. The man then turned and stepped into the woods.

Da Daa Pearls first words sounded out across the clearing. Pearl slid down from the safety of her mothers lap and ran to the center of the clearing. Her tiny footsteps striking the dust mingling with Corals large boot prints. Pearls head bent down, chin to heaving little chest, and she began to sob. Oma Da; Oma Da Daa; Pearl chanted over and over. Oma Da; Oma Da Daa; Knowing there was nothing she could do about Pearl or Coral, Rose went into the cabin to save super. Candle light is not true functional lighting, but a mere relief from total darkness. Anyone that has had to rely on candle flame for anything other than romancing wont give favor to it.

Rose sat on the warm hearth stone in the dimly lit cabin. She had added more water to the soup, and sat listening to Pearls cries. She stirred the soup with a long handled wooden spoon. Her heart felt heavy: she loved Pearl. They had grown close, though when Pearl was born times were mighty hard. Rose kept stirring.

Storms would rage tonight. Pearl wanted her father and Rose knew that this was not something she could moderate, control, or repair. Pearl's haunting first words carried away on the North Wind. Oma Da, Oma Da Da!

#NINETEEN#

The North Wind thrashed the branches of the North Pines. The North woods always dark, were very dark and becoming darker. It was not night but the dark of night descended and the smell of damp earth permeated the air. Menacing wind tossed the tops of the tall pines, but down under the air was still, dark, and heavy.

The North Wind carried Pearls cries through the tops of the tall pines, and on down through the town square. Dust clouds 6 ft.—n—more whipped and spiraled in the four corners of main street McDonough. The General store's afternoon social club ran for their horses. Thunder boomed, lightening arced and lit the sky. The wooden Indian took the bolt of lightning straight to his heart. Later on Ol Tuck drilled a hole clean through the old Indian and ran a bolt in from shoulder to shoulder to hold his left side on.

Out back in his favorite smoke hole, little Hattie had just took a big ol puff off real dry cigrett. The North Wind whipped the hot end off the cigrett into little Hattie's hair and burnt a three inch bald place on top of his head before he had time to bend over and run his head in the dirt.

Ol Tuck hovered in the middle of his store, head down on his knees prayin to "God" to forgive anything he ever done, might say, or think, or do in the future. Mostly he'd not mess around the North Woods no more. Many a North Pine child had the charismatic eye of Ol Tuck.

#TWUNTY#

The air in the North Woods did not stir, but hung close, the still air smelt of damp earth and old moss. The transition in stepping from the sunlit brightness of the clearing to the deep darkness of the piney woods was dramatic. The Old Man never heard Pearl cry out, for the impenetrable North Woods were just that impenetrable. Sound and wind carried through the tops of the tall pines, but never reached down into the dark depths where The Old Man now wandered lost.

He fell twice, and stumbled blindly, arms out before him knowing that he was in serious trouble. He muttered to himself rules about what to do if you are lost in some damn dark, creepy, woods. Ya; sit down, save energy, keep yerself warm with leaves or somethin. First off set down en stay put. He kept on stumbling around until he fell.

Falls are further in the dark than they are in the light. He thought he had stepped off the edge of the earth. He could see nothing stumbling through the woods, and when he stepped off flat land he dropped, rolled, and slid, down a nasty embankment. Blind, and unprepared, he had no way to keep from bouncing down the hill or any way to keep from crashing into trees, brush, and rocks. His bruised and battered body lay at the bottom of the hill eyes wide open, but seeing nothing.

#TWUNTY ONE#

Rose placed the lid carefully back on the iron soup pot, stood and stepped outside. She stood outside on the large flat stone step. Her bare feet took in the heat from the sun baked stone, but her heart chilled, at hearing the cries of her baby.

Pearl stood in the clearing sobbing: Oma Da, Oma Da Daa. Her little body shook, her cries were becoming weaker, and soon she just stood there. Her arms hung limply at her sides, her head bent forward, and she stared forlornly at the ground.

Rose saw Pearls shoulders droop in defeat, and couldn't stand it any longer. She ran to Pearl, knelt upon the ground and pulled her tiny sobbing baby into her arms. Nuzzling close the baby took an offered breast, while her mother rocked gently, sang softly, and the two of them effectively shut out the world.

#TWUNTY TOO#

His workin day was drawin to an end. For Ol Tuck the day'd been bout the same as any other. Until he'd slid the bolt home when closin up the store. Standin on the store porch, watchin the sun dip down, he took notice of the difernt colors in the sky up over the tree line. Reds, pinks, an a odd shade of deep violet had been spread smooth like, over a deep blanket of real dark blue.

When the bolt slid home he'd got a pricklin feelin, an a most urgent pull to get up to the woods. These premonent tweaks happened to him sometimes. Best not to mess about with premonents. Ol Tuck hurried off the store porch and stepped it lightly on home.

Ol Tuck, done mullin over the worrisome premonention, hitched up the heavy pack on his back, pulled his hat brim low, and takin long strides disappeared into the dark night.

Head down to the wind picking up force, Ol Tuck pushed onward. Keeping to the wagon track for a good patch of the way, he kept up a fairly steady stride, hardly losen time. Wasn't any reason for him to hurry but the premonent pull pushed at him. Drat if I aint gettin in to deep into I don't even know what I'm gettin in to.

It wasn't enuf with the wippin wind, now came rain, to go with the tormentuos flying debris slappin about, slowin the progress, to wherever he was goin. Ol Tuck followed his feet. It don't need to bluster ever time I take to go out of doors do it? Up the town road, onto the Creek road, and up the hill to the North Woods. Slipping around humps of upended earth and trees seeming to have grown into each other. Picking his way carefully through endless tangles of overgrown briars, he made his way into the forested depths of the North Wood.

#TWUNTY THUREE#

Rose sat in the clearing on the wet ground. She held Pearl close to her body keeping her warm and shielding the baby from the rain. They presented a dreary forlorn sight. Ol Tuck stood at the edge of the clearing soaking wet and tired.

His premonition had led him clear out here in the pitch dark of night in a tyrannical storm. Puzzled he called out to the woman. Hey lady; why er ya out here in the rain? The woman and the baby were soaked to the skin, and blended well with the muddied ground. Rivulets of rain ran from the woman's long hair, and her dress hem was indistinguishable in the mud. It was a sorry sight.

It was somethin else, the mother with head and shoulders bent, shielding her baby from harm. Ol Tuck thought to himself; she aint just keeping that kid warm she's a guardin it.

Ol Tuck feared no woman, never had, but he was no fool and bypassed the strange woman to go see what was wrong with the cabin. Why aint they in under shelter? The cabin door was a gapin wide open. With a caution he poked his head in around the door frame.

Food cooked over a dieing fire. Dumping his heavy pack off in a corner, he lifted the lid off the soup pot. The stuff smelt real good and he stirred it with a long handled spoon left laying on the hearth stone. He put the lid back and stoked up the fire. He saw no reason for the people to stay outside, so he went outside and looked to where Rose sat hunched and drenched.

Ol Tuck was wet, hungry, and had better plans in his mind than rescuing strangers and was quite direct. He stood on the porch step and ordered Rose to get up off her crazy hind and get inside: Now! He really hoped she could hear and think cause he didn't want to carry or drag her and she was comin inside.

Rose lifted her head, her long tresses of auburn hair draped soddenly across her cheek. Her muddy hand left dirty streaks on her wet face when she pushed her hair back. She tried to stand and fell back to the muddy earth. The baby was too heavy and the woman's skirts clung to her legs soggy, clinging, tripping her and she fell.

When Rose fell floundering helplessly, Ol luck jumped off the stone step in a rush to help her. His feet sank ankle deep in muck and mired him fast. aaahhh; He swayed and unable to move his feet they pulled on out of his boots as the top of him splayed into the muck.

Fire light shown out the cabin door and seeing it the chickens on the roof guessed to be morning. Wet fluff less chikins half asleep began stepping off the roof. They plopped down into the muddy yard squawking and flapping. Unable to walk in the deep mud they rolled about looking like something evil straight up from Hades.

The North Wind thrashed through the tall pines as Ol Tuck hauled himself up off the ground clawing and slinging mud as if he were spooked by creeping flopping demons. He stumbled over to Rose and pulled her to her feet. Her dress was water logged and heavy. Ol Tuck grabbed the dress at its neck line and tore it from neck to waste. The ruined dress dropped to the ground. He bootless, she dressless, they made haste to the safety of the cabin.

Pearl however stood knee deep in the mud, waving her little arms, pointing her tiny finger, and laughing, like it was a sunny day in May. A ray of light shown from the end of her tiny finger, and cast out an eerie beacon into the dark stormy night sky.

#TWUNTY FORE#

The Old Man lay very still not sure if he was still of one piece. The ray of light shining over his face was blinding after being so long in the pitch dark. He shut his eyes, opened them and pushed himself up right. Enough already: he wanted to go home. Covered with debris, scratched and sitting on hard ground, his head hurt, he was scratched, bruised, lost, and he shivered.

A ray of light shown once more over his face. Yer aint crippled get up an walk. He blinked. I caint haul ya home; get up an walk. It was the little gal that had been playing with Pearl on the creek bank.

The Old Man hurt from head to toe, was cold, hungry, and very tired. Yer a bossy little thing aint ya! Ef ya want to stay here keep on settin there cause I'm goin now. The little dark haired girl turned and started walking away.

Those eyes, and that air about her were familiar some way. The Old Man scrambled up and followed her he would figure out where he knew her someplace better than here. As he stumbled along behind the child he pondered to himself,. I'm following a child in the dark of night in the forest; aint there any parents livin up here?

The child stopped turned and pointed her glowing finger at him. Yes sir my mama is behind of you. Mind reading, an magic; gee wizikers, beyond wonderment he kept stumbling along. He never even turned his head to see if anyone followed him. The mother motioned for the child to continue.

#TWUNTY FIVE#

Ol Ma Hattie awoke in the night with a start. The drumming sound of rain on the roof was steady. But there was another sound, the snapping and cracking of fire, a big fire. She jumped from her soft feather bed, and night gown tails a flying ran out of her dry one room house straight into the storm.

She ran for the fire bell on the General Store but couldn't get to it. The back half of the store blazed high and furious, impervious to the blasting rain storm. Not able to use the bell Ol Ma used her voice for good for once in her life. She shrieked and called from the McDonough crossroads until everyone bailed from their beds, and came running to help.

They all came the whole town in answer to Ol Ma's calling out. The Biros, Bruers, Shattoks, Gipsons, Nightengail, Franky, and from afarther off Ol Bene. Some came on horse back, some in wagons, but most were afoot running with boots in hand. Water buckets passed from hand to practiced hand barely losing any water. The hot selfish fire claimed the entire store. When the bucket brigade finally collapsed in the street the only thing left of the McDonough General Store was the front palisade and the porch. The wooden Indian stood firm and proud though soot blackened and featherless.

The fire brigade dreaded the morning when they discovered that Ol Tuck was missing. At daylight they'd have to sort the remains of the store. But for the rest of the night: what there was left of it; they all prayed in their own fashion that Ol Tuck was someplace else.

#TWUNTY SIX#

Huddled shivering, Rose sat on the hearthstone wrapped in a huge fur. Ol Tuck stirred up the fire and added only the driest wood to it making the fire take fast and throw heat.

Silhouetted by the light of the open cabin door was little Pearl. She stood barefoot upon the cold stone step. The beacon from her tiny finger held high shining out into the stormy sky. Ol Tuck and Rose had dragged her kicking and fighting to the step, and with threats of tying her down if she left the stone, let her have her own way.

The little dark haired girl raised her arm and pointed her tiny finger upward toward what would heave been the heavens in a forest clearing. The light that shone strangely from the child's finger found its way up through the dense forestation above finding another. Shining bright: one eerie beam a beacon, steadfast in the storm, guiding the second little wandering beam bearer to safety.

#TWUNTY SEVUN#

Ol Ma Hattie was once more at the crossroads of McDonough. Except this time she was on her knees head in hands, sobbing and praying to God. She had gone home after the fire and ready to collapse had found her son little C.G. gone. Little Tommy lay curled, his thumb in his mouth, alone, in the tiny trundle bed belonging to the brothers.

Rain splashed down around her kneeling form and she cried as only a mama with a lost child can. On the porch of the McDonough General Store the life size wooden Indian watched over her. His all seeing eyes not able to tell her good news or bad.

#TWUNTY ATE#

The North Wind howled with fury, as the night carried on. Little Pearl ignored the cold stone under her bare feet, until Oma Da Da issued forth quietly one last time, from tiny heart shaped lips. Pearl, exhausted, sank slowly and lay upon the cold stone step.

Ol Tuck firmly pressed Rose's shoulder with a big hand. Stay at the fire, thaw yerself. I ken look out fer the babe. Rose's mother heart quickened a beat, but she stayed and let Ol Tuck go tend to Pearl. He lifted another fur off the bed, dumping over a small woven basket.

Rose stared at the upset basket on the bed. The objects strewn carelessly about the bed were tokens. Each token held a specific connotation. Each small stone was a key, to rainfall, plant growth, and animal population. Some of the tiny figures guarded the edges of the North Woods. When in their proper place the homely, but powerful little figures were not a large threat. In the wrong or untrained hand McDonough and surrounding properties faced drought, flooding, lightening, fire, over growth, no growth, and wind, wild, wild wind. These simple carved figures were also keys that could bind or separate forever, wood folk and town folk.

Outside on the stone step Ol Tuck carefully lifted Pearl cradling her in his arms. He sat on the edge of the step with the bear skin fur draped over his head. Sich a teeny little gal ya are ta try ta save yer ol man. I'll hep ya what I ken bitty one. Ol Tuck held Pearls tiny had in his big one. Once again a steady beacon of light shone far out into the night sky.

Seventeen; I hope there are still seventeen pieces. Rose sat neked on the bed. The fur she'd been wrapped in had slid from her shoulders and had no priority in her thoughts just now. She carefully placed the tokens back into the woven basket. Fourteen were all she found before she started stripping the bed and shaking the furs. The tokens were gone. Rose shivered with a chill that had naught to do with cold.

#TWUNTY NINE#

Old Bene slopped along the narrow path that led to his farm. His boots were lost now. They was in his hands on the way to the fire, but he never got time to shove his feet into them. He guessed his feet had better tough up cause they ud be naked till the store got replaced and got restocked.

It was just a little hill yet it seemed to be the slickest part of the whole damn path. Old Bene's feet slipped two steps back for every small step forward. He tried running up the slippery hill with a short burst, flailing his arms for balance. Churning his bare feet, his toes digging in for grippage he spun quickly up the little hill. He stopped at the top to get his wind back.

Old Bene coughed and wheezed and sorely considered layin down to die. He then looked up at the driving rain; down at the mud; and said he'd be damned if this hell wouldn't out due the other one and headed on home.

Something was a stirring in the leafy brush alongside the narrow path. In a storm wild as this one all the wild animals would be hunkered down snug and safe someplace. That left sick animals, spooks, an dumb humans outdoors, something was to brainless to get in out a the rain.

Never breaking stride at the place where he heard the noise in the bushes Old Bene reached in the bushes, quickly with a long arm and a big hand. With a powerful swat swipe he yanked out the trouble. The noise was now visible and audible. Little C.G. Hattie screamed at the end of Old Bene's arm.

Little Hattie kicked voylently an Old Bene swung him around so's he could see the kids face. Still walking he spoke the boy in a most serious tone. Enough noise boy! Why ya way out here? Be a good idee to answer soon afore I get way on home. I got a feelin your in some deep dung boy and there's a broad strop a hangin at the house with yer name on it.

Little Hattie begun screamin an kickin an thrashin voylently. Old Bene grabbed the boy with both hands an started runnin real fast down the path. Old Bene started sing songin loud a sayin: What ya do boy? Mamas not here boy. What ud ya do boy? Old Bene's gonna thrash ya good. Little Hattie thinkin he was really gonna die begun to bawl. I dint do it. The store burnt itself. I aint been smoking. I want my mama. I waannnt mmyyy maamaaaa!

Old Bene's bare foot stomped on something rough an he howled out a blast of ungodly language. He and little Hattie's screaming an cursin woke Mrs. Bene. Mrs. Bene was sure that major demons were on the loose. So she took the old double barrel sawed off down off its hook over the door.

Rain eased off the eves of the Bene homestead in arching torrents. Her feet shoved sockabare into oversized barn boots Mrs. Bene stood on her front porch in her night dress listening for peculerareities in the noise of the raging storm. She had decided that the demons were human, but she didn't put the gun away, just held the big blaster cradled in her arms.

Old Bene nursed his injured foot, by hopping around on his other one. This was fine until he hopped onto something else. Then he an the boy slipped and crashed headlong into the sloppin muddy path.

In a frenzy little Hattie scrabbled around in the mud diggin an a clawin tryin to get away. He got to his feet but Old Bene flat out in the muck reached out a long skinny arm and yanked the kid back down by the ankle.

Little Hattie screamed like to diein an started kicken, thrashin, and slingin mud. Old Bene hauled his mud drippin body up off the ground. He not so kindly hauled little Hattie up by his shirt neck, squeezed him a bit, and resumed his trek for home.

The demons were sneakin up on Mrs. Bene. They weren't screaming now but she just knew they were getting close. The buckshot blast from the sawed off took out most of the porch rail and lit up the whole yard for a split second. Old Bene dove back of the wood stack saving his own hide fallin heavily onto the temporarily forgotten little boy.

Rolling off little Hattie, Old Bene put his large hand over the kids mouth an whispered to him ef ya got any brains keep yer yap shut that explosion was a scared womin in the dark handling a gun.

Lookin up wide eyed at Old Bene Little C.G. Hattie reached up and pulled Old Bene's hand away from his mouth. He whispered out "brains" Yer the one left the damn gun loaded.

Behind the woodpile the man and the boy lay unmoving for quite a spell. Hard rain drumming down was the only sound, nothing more sounded from the dark Bene homestead.

Stiff and bone chilled from layin on wet gnarly ground back o the wood pile for most of the night, Old Bene pushed himself up. C'mon kid; I'm goin in; I'm darn cold and hungry. With great caution Old Bene peeked over the top row of wood. Ma he called out: where are ya at? Ready to duck-n-cover he waited; listening. Barefoot an pickin his way through shrapnel, wooden splinters of what had once been his porch Old Bene made his way to his house.

Morning sun creeping over the desecrated porch revealed Mrs. Bene feet first, legs and arms splayed akimbo. Mrs. Bene lay sprawled knocked out colder than a yesterday's biscuit from the powerful force of the sawed off. Old Bene raced barefoot up the litter strewn path, ignoring the debris. Ma—Ma—Get up Ma.

Running along behind Old Bene, little Hattie followed the panicked man back tracking the path taken just hours ago. Slung up over her husbands shoulder Mrs. Bene in her flannel nightdress and large rubber boots bounced along. Her husband thinking she was dead or diein ran for town fast as he was able.

#THURTY#

The Old Man stumbled and nearly fell over a large tree root. Aurianna giggled and her mother shushed her. He is merely a man; the mother admonished the child just light the way, and stop teasing him. He cant see in the dark like us. Lets get him home before he falls down and hurts himself worse. Aurianna unwrapped her hand from her dress and light shone once again on the thick pine covered woodland floor.

Don't worry Coral, you'll get home. Ok. Rose is waiting for you. The Old Man stopped walking and turned around. He regarded a woman nearly as beautiful as his Rose. He did not speak, he merely shook his head, turned about and went back to stumbling after the little girl.

Coral if you have questions or something to say you ought to quit the shy stuff. Have you not already muffed about for half your life trying to figure stuff out on your own.

The Old Man stopped walking once again, but this time he did not turn around. Leonesia walked past him and stopped. Well now what? She stated firmly. Aurianna wait for us. Aurianna was tired; the day had been long, so she sat down on the ground to rest her little legs. Two beams of light in the night sky had now vanished leaving the night incredibly black.

Leonesia snapped her fingers and sparkling lights lit up the glen. The sparkly lights flickered and danced much like fire flies of a summer eve.

How much mind reading can ya all do? Do all women know how dumb I am? I caint stay here. I caint go home. He knelt down, one knee on the red earth, What'd I ever leave my house for? Now I don't even got one.

Whoa now; Mr. Phillips; Leonesia spoke sternly to Coral as she pointed her finger at his face. Did you ever stop to think; that it could be; that you, are not the only one up here abouts in a royal predicament. For added emphasis she poked him directly between his eyes with a dentful force.

Ow! Well quit blattin and keep walking we have much to do. I will answer your questions on the way.

The forest glen shimmered, sparkling tiny lights flickered, and shone underneath the thick pine boughs, as would stars in a clear night sky. Aurianna lay curled, head on folded hands, sleeping sweetly. Leonesia meant to awaken her. She tapped the child's shoulder, but Aurianna merely squirmed a bit and curled up tighter.

Leonesia tried to carry Aurianna but the sleeping child was far to heavy. The Old Man took the little girl from her mother and they continued on. The little girl snugged up to him and with her head resting on his shoulder he found himself missing Pearl; a lot.

The night waned and morning sun filtered down through the pines onto the heads of The Old Man, the child's head nestled on his shoulder, and the blond head of Leonesia. It seemed this night would last forever. The Old Man shifted Aurianna's head onto his other shoulder. He was going to ask Leonesia about the mind reading, but they were back at the clearing.

#THURTY ONE#

Pearl stirred in Ol Tucks arms. She peeked out from under the dripping fur. What ya about little one. Pearl turned her curly blond sleep tousled head and looked intently up at Ol Tuck with her big green eyes. `Oma Da" she said.

Ol Tuck pushed the wet fur off. The rain had stopped, stars shown brightly as the storm clouds slowly wafted off. Wet bear fur lay on the cold slate stone step in a heap, discarded, its usefulness past. The spent storm clouds wafted off, grey dawn slid over the clearing, revealing scenes of the nights stormy tempest.

On the step Ol Tuck sat next to little Pearl, whilst Rose, nekid, stood behind the two of them. The three exhausted people watched the grey clouds pass, the warm sun rise, and quietly contemplated puffs of steam lifting from the puddle covered clearing.

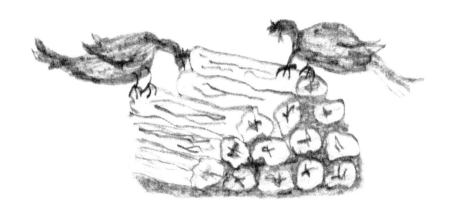

The mud demons, spooks of the night now perched in brown blobs on the wood pile trying to dry themselves out. The torn dress lay in a heap where it had fallen and torn as it was, it was the only dress Rose owned. She'd have to wash and mend it. Ol Tucks boots stood tall and proud stuck upright just where they'd been firmly planted in the muck.

Pearl wandered off the step and was pokin at the chikins. Click-clikin at the sorry looking birds, while she poked at them with her finger. Rose pulled her dress up out of the mud, and interrupting Pearls play, took her by the hand and started down the path to the Gene.

Mind if I help you? The first thing to meet his eyes was Rose in all her glory! "WOW"! what a way to step into a new life. Her long auburn hair hung over her back past her knees, and almost covered her, but not quite.

Ol Tuck put his fingers to his lips and made a motion with his hand for The Old Man to continue, and excused himself in the same motion.

Ol Tuck grinned, and Leonesia slapped his behind playfully. How about if we all go wash up. Some of us smell like trackers that have been up all night.

Leonesia laughed as Ol Tuck nudged her with intent. Ol Tuck took Aurianna's hand, and with an arm around his girl passed by Rose and Pearl, where the two stood standing awe struck in the clearing.

Coral; oh I missed you so bad. Coral removed his shirt placed it around Rose's shoulders, and holding the arms of the shirt tightly in his fists pulled her close. Next time that I act like an ass, would ya kindly tell me to eat oats or something.

#THURTY TOO#

Ol Ma Hattie lay curled on her side. Worn out with grief and worry she lay at the crossroad of McDonough sound asleep. An old dog loped down the dirt road early of the morning. He stopped to sniff at her ear, but she snored on. He kicked a bit of dirt at her with his hind foot and continued about his travels.

Being left to raise her two boys Tommy and C.G. over and often was trying on itself. Being scared to the death by the fierce unforgiving fire took more starch from her, but the idee of losin one of her dearest sapped her to her very bones. She slept through soundly when the sun came over the hill.

#THURTY THUREE#

Ahhhh-sploosh: Probly somewhere in the grand earth there is a swimming hole that a body could wade into, the Gene is not one of them. Cold cant quite get a grip on the below degree facter.

Leonesia reached the shore line first and balked at the waters edge. Ol Tuck running up behind her, grabbed her, and tossed her over his shoulder. Got to be true love to be doused into the fridged water of the Gene, come up for air and laugh.

Coral and Rose hand in hand, feet in sand, looked each other in the eye, been said a time or two the sun could shine fer a month on that particular creek an never touch a lick of the frost in it. Well best not to contemplate on it. The two lovers dove off the sandy bank. Huhhhhh—coming up for air after the shock on their bodies the four people swam about like mad dogs tryin to get used to the water temprature.

Two little girls played quietly in the shade entertaining themselves with three tiny little stone dolls. Talking little girl gibberish, caught up in a world of fanciful thinking, the children sat upon the soft green moss of the creek bank mindless of the antics of their swimming parents

Leonesia helped Rose to wash the mud out of her dress. The two women perched immodestly on large warm rocks inches above the water line. The two were taking turns slapping the dirty wet dress onto moss free rocks in the cold creek.

Oh Rose; this dress is a wreck. I'll try to help you sew it together, but it may be prime time to get some yard goods. Leonesia's voice relayed her doubts about resurrecting Roses old torn dress.

This dress will have to do, for I haven't got another one, and yard goods cost money. Rose really would have liked a new dress, hope did shine in her eye, for a twinkle of a second.

Aw did you see that? I just have to get that women to town. She's been denied the right of a beautiful woman. The right to proper love and care, and I did it to her. Why'd I let her go off Tuck? I should have known better than that.

Don't beat yerself up now, Old Man. Yuv got her back, so lets get her to town. I have some changes to think on, regardin my own lost freedom just now. Ol Tuck gazed at the ladies, working so hard to fix the unfixable. Wonder why women work so hard at fixin things? Things that's gone beyond, trying to keep us men together, house and home, kids, animals. Must feel like paddlin up river with a match stick at times.

Hedgerows, stone walls, and red dirt, all sure signs of the best land on earth, of home land, heart, and soul. Home is not just a place to be, it is an ingrained such, that comes from living. Home life is the living that goes past without the seeing of it.

When it came to be time to go, Pearl put a small carved figure into each of Aurianna's pockets, and held a third firmly in her own little hand. They all came out of the dark woods, Ol Tuck, Leonesia, The Old Man, Rose, and the children Aurianna and little Pearl. Out through a part in the tangle of briars, onto the red dirt road they walked heading for town. The men carried the children and the women led the way out of darkness into the light.

Two rain soaked willows at the very edge of the North Woods tipped, entwining, leaves, branches, and trunks, creating a gnarly tangled barrier along the woodsman's path. New green shoots pushed tiny sprouts from the damp dark earth. These tiny plants would soon create a mass tangle of thorny brambles impenetrable to most any being except rabbits. And on the far side of the North Woods the ground heaved and large stones rolled effectively into place blocking any reasonable passage in or out. Three talisman's granting passage, now missing.

#THURTY FORE#

Wet flannel pulled at Mrs. Bene's bruised flesh. Half awake, she opened her eyes wider. She then closed them quickly praying with a fervor that she was in the midst of a nightmare. Pulling at the neckline of her nightgown which was definitely soaked, she slowly opened her eyes and accepted the facts.

The ache in her back was from the hitching pole, which her body was propped against. She made no noise in hopes that the town folk gathering in chattering groups nearby would not know she lay in hoof dirt of horse in her altogether.

Her eyes registered wonderment at the scene before her. A crowd was gathering in front of the remains of the McDonough General Store. Smoke puffed up periodically behind the smoke blackened wooden Indian. Tired looking men carried rakes and shovels and Mrs. Bene wondered, Why?

Over in the road her husband Old Bene and little C.G. Hattie were pulling Ol Ma Hattie's prone form from the center lane by her dress hem. A bit indelicate. Was she dead? No; she was quite well and she grabbed up her little son with a flourish.

Mama, mama, what are ya doin out here? Panting for breath little hobnailed boots had pounded the dirt of the narrow dirt road. Little

Hattie had run to his mother, scared to death she'd died in the street or something.

Awakened suddenly, thoroughly alarmed at being hauled about by her dress tails, Ol Ma Hattie had kicked her feet voylently until she realized that her dear sweet son was safe. My son, My son, My little son. She'd wrapped her protecting mother arms around him and squuueeezed the precious child to her chest.

Listening to the men gathered about, Mrs. Bene discovered that the store keep was presumed dead in the ashes of the general store. After much discussion the McDonough General Porch Committee began to wander off to their assorted farms. Having decided to wait until the still hot store remains cooled off, before entertaining the gruesome task of digging out Ol Tucks bones.

Smelling smoke, Leonesia, and Rose, looked at each other with much concern on their faces and put some speed in their step. The small group traveling along the narrow creek road was nearing town.

Each person in the small group approached the McDonough town square with his, or her, own apprehensions. Leonesia and her sister Rose had been gone about three years or four, The Old Man but three weeks, Ol Tuck had unthinkably abandoned his store, and for the little girls this was true adventure.

#THURTY FIVE#

All heads at the McDonough four corners turned at the arrival of the small odd entourage. Quite a picture they did present. Leonesia, tall, blond, and lovely, Rose dressed in a still damp dress, covered by the old mans shirt, which left him, bare of chest. The little girls hung back, afraid at so many new faces and Ol Tuck stopped dead in his tracks.

Mrs. Bene watched both groups with interest. The towns people stood about looking stunned for a minute, and then very slowly, started stomping, their feet hitting the bare ground hard, toward the woodland folk. Being stomped at, the woodland folk took a step back.

Ow, ow, ow, holding the post of the hitching rail, Mrs. Bene pulled her aching body up off the ground. She leant there watching the groups standing about in what seemed to have become a face off. Might they fight? She did not know and began to worry. Children were present, these grown people should be careful.

Stepping to the front of the stomping pack, Ol Ma Hattie lead the towns people, confronting the woods folk. Ol Ma began to chant at the new comers, others picked up the rhythm. Trouble makers, fire starters, get back, get back.

Get back, go home, trouble makers, fire starters, get back go home. Following Ol Ma's lead the towns people approached Coral, Ol Tuck,

Rose, and Leonesia. Aurianna and little Pearl peeked from behind their mothers skirts. Aurianna's face puckered, the little girl was near tears, Pearl however scowled.

The North Wind became quiet. Pearl stomped her tiny foot on the hard earth. The air was instantly filled with swooping birds. Pearl whistled and the ground was filled with darting, chittering ground squirrels. Ol Ma Hattie stomped a step closer to Pearl.

The North Wind resumed its song, whistling a warning. The town people stood stunned wondering if perhaps this was a bad idea.

Cautiously Ol Ma took a step closer to Pearl. Pearl's chin came up. Ol Ma took another step toward Pearl. Pearls big green eyes flashed a warning. Pearl raised her arm, her tiny hand turning slowly.

Pearly: Her father said sternly, while clapping his big hands loudly. Pearl stopped instantly and looked at her father. Oma Da? He reached down and picked Pearl up. He hugged her close to himself as he raised his hand palm outward and moved toward the crowd threatening his friends and family.

This is how it will be from here to forever. Back up and go about your business. If ya town folk are in a feudin mood go feud about with yourselves. These here women and little babies are goin to live here in McDonough.

Heads dropped in shame these were their friends. They couldn't be run out a town. The McDonough General Stores Porch Committee turned on Ol Ma Hattie. Knowing it was of no use to tell her what to do they merely crowded her in. Ol Ma found herself smushed between the large bodies of Gipson, Franky, Bruer, and the banker Mr. Nightengail.

She couldn't see over their heads, and she was to cramped to speak, so she gave up and was quiet.

Two faced as rotten as ya are, Ol Ma Hattie I am sure that you can put on a show of welcome to my wife, my child, and my friends. I found out some neat stuff while I was away in them back woods and unless you really, really, want to see fire fly, back up, and do it quick.

Don't know if that were bravo or bull Old Man? Look at them men, all with rakes and shovels.

Don't know Tuck? But they backed off. Lets go see what happened to your store.

Wood folk stood once more surrounded by townspeople. Together the crowd stood facing the smoldering ashes of what had held the community together. The smoke blackened wooden Indian stared back at the crowd. There was not much else to see, other than the Indian. The mood was no longer tense with anger or fear of the unknown. The tides had come about to sadness, loss of Ol Tucks store was not just his loss, but a loss affecting everyone in the town, as well as the many outside travelers.

Leonesia held tight to Ol Tucks hand. Together they stood watching puffs of hot ash and smoke flitt off on the breeze.

Hey Tuck! We sure are glad thet yer not dead. Didn't know ya was a datin even, and now ya got a whole family. Put a tag on one an ya got a let em in the house. Aint thet just sompthin else.

Well I'm glad ya showed yerself back home. Shoveling aint good for me back an yer alive so we'd a been diggin all day fer nothing.

Don't look so decrepit we're all here to help build up a new store. The Indians still whole that's a good sign.

The Indian looked back at the people with his all seeing eye. Hot ash puffed up from behind the all seeing wooden Indian and was then carried off on a short gusty breeze. Yet as usual he kept his insights, ponderings, and amusements of the towns happenings to himself.

Having been through a half dozen growth spurts in one night little Hattie weren't so little no more. The fact that Old Bene had spared his backside a well deserved beating left him some dignity and he decided to repay the act with a life long resolve. He would never—ever smoke again!

A marvel it was, standing tall, how it got there no one knew. Whatever powers put it back, put it on the wrong side of the road. No one ever did find out how the McDonough General Store got rebuilt in the dark of night.

The North Wind carried its timeless message through the cross roads of McDonough N.Y. The all seeing Indian looked on with nary a word and yet seemed he to smile. Where bafore this, every morning's dawn of his carved wooden life he'd been ever so stern.

#THURTY SIX#

The little girl hugging her knees on the porch step turned the stone in her hand about with wonder. The stone was warm and she rubbed the dirt off it. Why it looked just kinda like a tiny man. Kinda like the stones grandma had stored away in the small wooden box in under her bed. She'd have to wait till grandma was busy, she'd never been told not to play with the 14 little stones, she just had a powerful feeling that she should not.

Twitchy twitch, the pesky summer fly buzzed off lifting lazily from the lumpy dogs brown fuzzy ear. Rays of warm sun baked the wide slat porch floor. The old curly haired dog stretched his legs out making the effort look taxing. Hugo opened one eye, closed it, perked an ear, relaxed his limbs and half listened to the afternoon porch committee as if to sum up the tales just told.

Na, from farmer Franky, cant be. Well said Gipson where does that darn giant buck disappear to? Ya I want to eat the sonabitch come huntin season. Shattock you cant even shoot straight, how ya gonna eat that buck live? Listen Junior Bruer I aim true every shot. Laughter on the porch carried out through the parking lot.

Nezbitt and Riteout, cars parked next to one other in the parking lot pointed index fingers at each other and nixed each other with a loud bang. Finding much humor on the comedy Wally Wats laughed himself clean over the porch rail.

I don't know about all the spooky stuff. Could be true but the only proof is in the North Woods, an I for one aren't going in them. Hey! Its getting late, almost six time for HEE HAW. Cant miss HEE HAW or Gun Smoke. See ya all tomorrow fellas. Dust swirled as Old Bob put motion into the straw broom cleaning his store porch with swift quick strokes. Closing time was closing time, to the minute.

Quiet Man Shoore gave a grunt which could either be taken for approval, or disapproval of the story, and then slowly moved off the porch. Strings of spiders web trailed him as he went. The lady spider most undeniably using spider swear at him after spending all after noon thinking he was a solid post scurried off to begin the process all over.

#THURTY SEVUN#

14 stones all in a box, lay in a row on a bed of dried moss. Carefully so carefully grubby little hands lifted the woven lid of the basket back. Chin on hand, elbow on polished wood floor, and careful not to hit her curly blond head on the wire bed springs above her, the little girl compared the 14 stones in the box to the one in her hand. I have a new friend for you tiny moss people. Here I'll stand you up. A proper greeting for a new guest. I will read to you from the book, while you all get to know each other.

Far off in the North Woods a huge buck led his small herd out a brand new passage. Trees had tipped, falling, rolling, crushing large tangles of sharp briars. Stepping with a caution the family of deer fed on the grass of the Phillips farm, while about them the North Wind whistled its eternal song.

The North Wind gently drew a wave through the curled white hair of Grandma Rose. The rocker ceased to rock on the wide front porch of the Phillips farm as the song of Grandma carried away in the music of the North Wind. We are one, part and parcel with the land, trees, and wood life.

CREDITS

THANK YOU ALL

TO: My Grandmothers,

Great, Great Grand Mother Meeker, She came to here from there, so can I.

Great Grandmother, Ethil Kalicicky, for giving to me a love of art.

Grandmother Elizabeth Crandall, for giving to me a love of the natural history.

Grandmother Mildred Phillips, for showing me how to love and be loved.

Grandmother Daisy Monroe, for showing me that a person can survive on the move.

Grandmother Millie Yerton, for letting me know that life is not so serious, fun is OK.

TO: My Mothers,

Mother Celia Yerton, for allowing me freedom of thought, and the insight to write it down.

Mother Vivian Phillips, for instituting a love of God.

TO: My Fathers,

Father Timothy Phillips, for making me a part of the red dirt back roads, the green of trees, and the dazzle of night stars.

Father Theodore Yerton, said to me, you can craft it, build it if you want it.

TO: My Sonny,

My Sonny Lauren, Thank you for carrying on the family tradition. Follow your heart. I LOVE YOU !

TO: My Sister Mildred, and My Brothers, Rob, Davey, Donald, Chuck, and Pork, for loving me no matter what. We are the magic 7.

TO: My Teachers,

Ann Moore, whom, of her own time taught me to read.

Mrs. Robb, Seeded a budding artist.

Mrs. Truman, Found some very well hidden writing potential.

Mrs. Snedecker, Put sunshine and color into my black world.

To My Ex David, for giving me space to write::: When he left me cold, hungry, and stranded I had plenty of time to think . . . .

And Thank You Linda Place for telling me to get the book out of the Drawer and publish it. It wont do any body any good in a drawer.

TO:

The People of The Community, For being UNIQUE.
NAMES HAVE BEEN CHANGED
TO PROTECT THE NONEXISTENT

BY
KIMBERLY ANN